Whei Came Home

By Delma-Venudi Geary
Art by Jay-R Pagud

Library For All Ltd.

When Talu Came Home

First published 2018
This edition published 2021

Published by Library For All Ltd
Email: info@libraryforall.org
URL: libraryforall.org

This book was previously produced by the Together For Education Partnership supported by the Australian Government through the Papua New Guinea-Australia Partnership.

This edition was made possible by the generous support of the Education Cooperation Program.

Original illustrations by Jay-R Pagud

When Talu Came Home
Geary, Delma-Venudi
ISBN: 978-1-922621-20-7
SKU01608

When Talu Came Home

Daddy always told me a story at bedtime.

But all that changed when Talu came home.

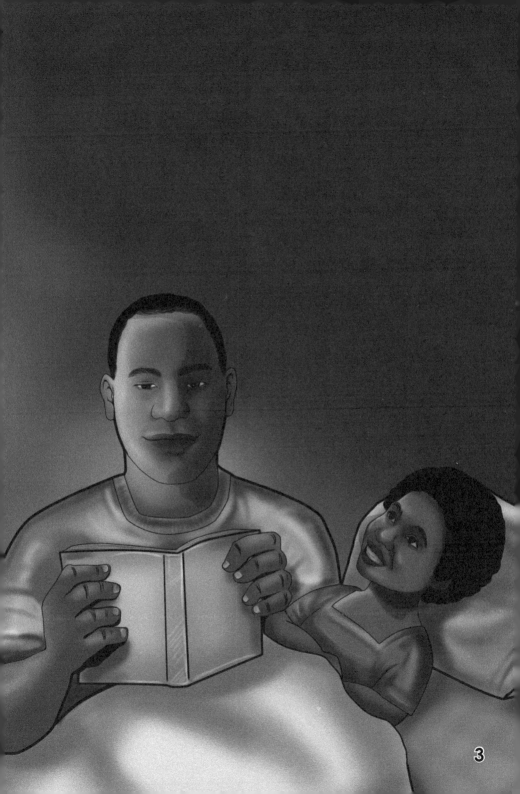

3

Mum always sang to me and rocked me to sleep.

But all that changed when Talu came home.

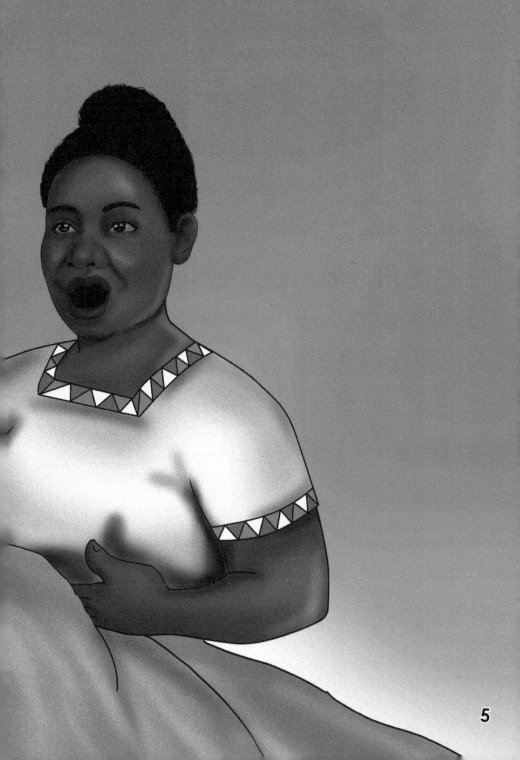

Grandmother always hugged me first when she came to visit.

But all that changed when Talu came home.

Grandfather always sat
me on his knee.

But all that changed
when Talu came home.

9

Now Daddy says, "Not now Wella," putting my book away.

Now Mum says, "Straight to bed Wella," and hurries off.

13

Grandmother says, "Keep out of the way, Wella," and her arms are always full.

And Grandfather never says much to me anymore, except "Wella, be quiet and sit still."

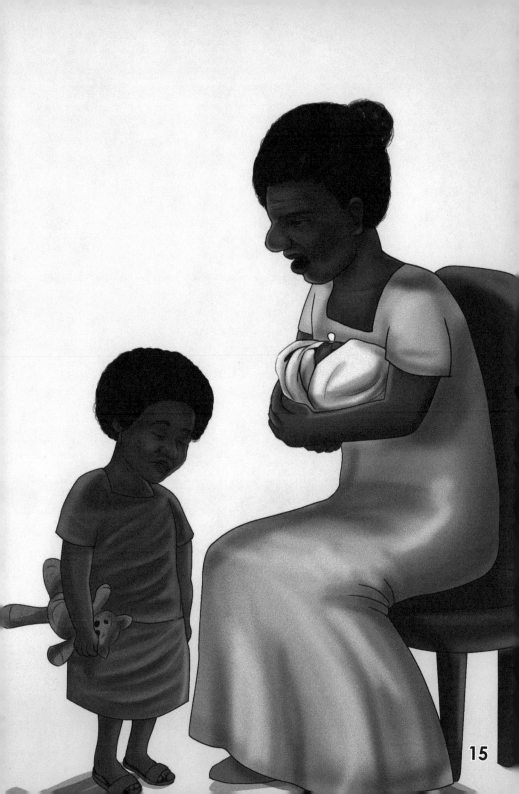

15

What's so special about Talu?

All he does is cry, eat and sleep. He is noisy and he smells!

"He is a baby," says Mum.

"He can't do anything for himself yet," says Grandmother

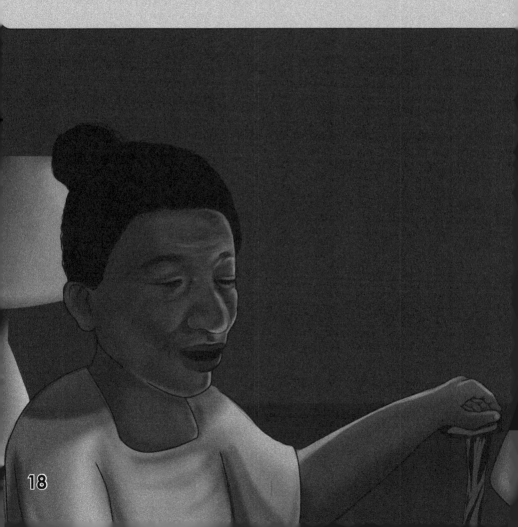

"You're a big girl now," says Grandfather.

"Most importantly, Wella, you are special and there is no one quite like you. You are a big sister."

"I am?" I say. "I don't feel very special since Talu came home."

"Yes," says Daddy, "and being a big sister means you are strong and smart. You can do so many good things all on your own! We are sorry for being so busy, but it does not mean that we don't love you too."

think about Daddy's words.

"Does that mean I can read to Talu and sing to him too?"

"Of course!" says Mum. "Talu would love that!" says Dad.

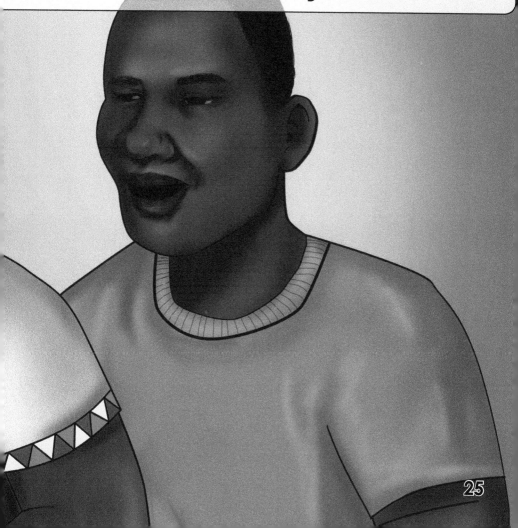

I give my family a huge smile and choose a book to read to Talu at bedtime. I am a very special big sister now.

And all that changed when Talu came home.

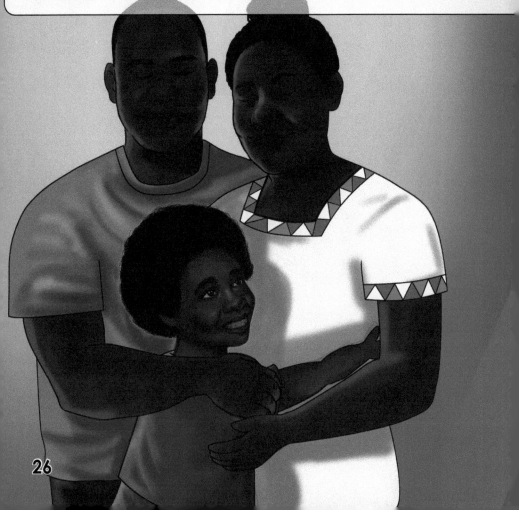

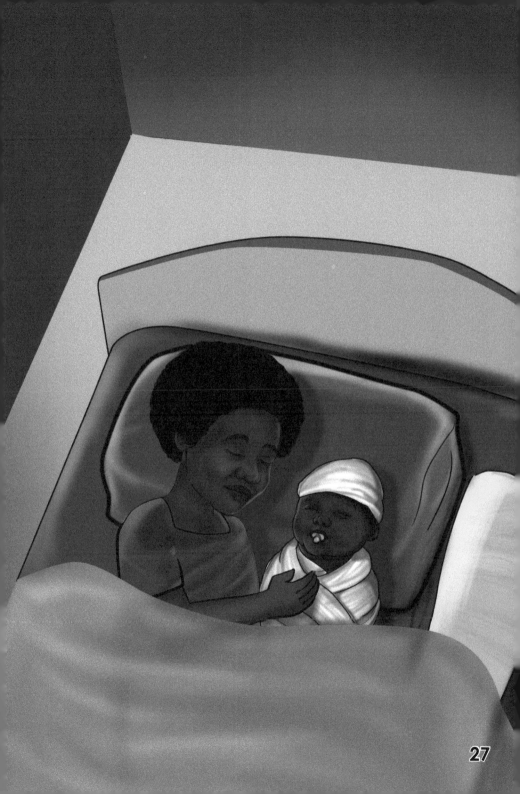

You can use these questions to talk about this book with your family, friends and teachers.

What did you learn from this book?

Describe this book in one word. Funny? Scary? Colourful? Interesting?

How did this book make you feel when you finished reading it?

What was your favourite part of this book?

download our reader app
getlibraryforall.org

About the contributors

Library For All works with authors and illustrators from around the world to develop diverse, relevant, high quality stories for young readers. Visit libraryforall.org for the latest news on writers' workshop events, submission guidelines and other creative opportunities.

Did you enjoy this book?

We have hundreds more expertly curated original stories to choose from.

We work in partnership with authors, educators, cultural advisors, governments and NGOs to bring the joy of reading to children everywhere.

Did you know?

We create global impact in these fields by embracing the United Nations Sustainable Development Goals.

libraryforall.org

CPSIA information can be obtained
at www.ICGtesting.com
Printed in the USA
BVHW051939080621
609012BV00012B/2387

9 781922 621207